WHOOPS! A HISTORY OF BAD DAYS

BAD DAYS IN
BATTLE

BY DON NARDO

ignite

CAPSTONE PRESS
a capstone imprint

Ignite is published by Capstone Press, an imprint of Capstone,
1710 Roe Crest Drive, North Mankato, Minnesota 56003
www.mycapstone.com

Library of Congress Cataloging-in-Publication Data
Names: Nardo, Don, 1947- author.
Title: Bad days in battle / by Don Nardo.
Description: North Mankato, Minnesota : Heinemann Raintree, an imprint of
    Capstone Press, [2017] | Series: Ignite. Whoops! A history of bad days |
    Includes bibliographical references and index. | Audience: Grades 4-6.
Identifiers: LCCN 2016031305l
ISBN 9781410985620 (library binding) |
ISBN 9781410985668 (eBook PDF)
Subjects: LCSH: Battles—Juvenile literature. | Military history—Juvenile
    literature.
Classification: LCC D25 .N38 2017 | DDC 355.4/8—dc23
LC record available at https://lccn.loc.gov/2016031305

Editorial Credits
Melissa York, editor; Nikki Farinella, designer and production specialist

Photo Credits
AP Images: PE, 36; Getty Images: Bettmann, 21, DeAgostini, 40, Hulton Archive/
Reinhold Thiele, 10, Roger Viollet, 9, UIG/PHA, 31; Glow Images: Heritage Images/The
Print Collector, 11; iStockphoto: f1monaco31, 38, Klaus Hollitzer, 24, Kolbz, 14, maisna,
39, swilmor, 17, VladislavStarozhilov, 13; Library of Congress: Prints and Photographs
Division, 4, 5, (all), 18, 19, 30, U.S. Army Signal Corps, 8; Newscom: Design Pics, 28,
Everett Collection, 32, 37, Heritage Images/The Print Collector, 33 (left), ITAR-TASS/Фото
ИТАР-ТАСС, 34, VWPics/Ken Ross, 20, ZB/picture alliance/euroluftbild.de, 25; North
Wind Picture Archives, 7, 35, Gerry Embleton, 6; Red Line Editorial, 16 (map); Shutterstock:
beibaoke, 23, Everett Historical, 5 (top), Fotokon, 26, PandaVector, 27 (bagpipes), Sean
Pavone, 5 (bottom), Sergey Goryachev, 33 (right), sharpner, 27 (bows, swords), terekhov
igor, 41, VoodooDot, 16 (soldier Icons); U.S. Air Force photo by Staff Sgt. Samuel Bendet,
cover; U.S. Coast Guard photo, 29; U.S. Department of Defense, 12; U.S. Navy: Naval
History and Heritage Command, 22

Design Element: Shutterstock Images: Designer things (bursts, dots, and bubble cloud)

Printed in Canada.
010035S17

TABLE OF CONTENTS

A VERY BAD DAY

SPECTACULAR FAILURES

Throughout recorded history, war has been largely a serious, bloody business. Mistakes are usually fatal. But sometimes blunders and other unexpected events occur that turn out to be outlandish, surprising, or just plain wacky. It has always been part of human nature to laugh at others' mistakes. Some past blunders made in wartime continue to tickle our funny bones despite the death and destruction always surrounding war.

General Burnside's glorious whiskers gave rise to the term "sideburns."

In 1862, during the American Civil War (1861–1865), Union general Ambrose Burnside let a little water stop him. He and his men needed to cross a river and wasted three hours looking for a ford. Eventually they crossed a well-guarded bridge and suffered heavy losses. The blunder? The river was shallow enough that they could have splashed across anywhere!

OOPS!

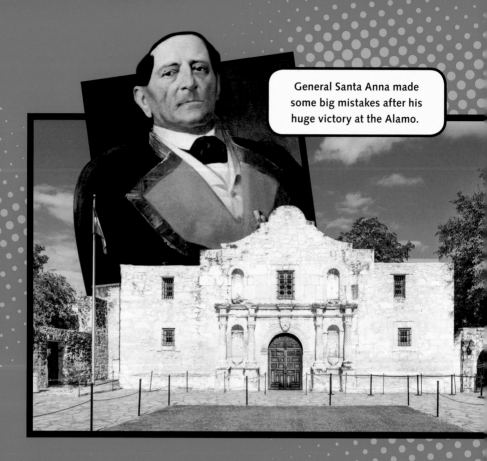

General Santa Anna made some big mistakes after his huge victory at the Alamo.

SLIPUPS ON THE SAN JACINTO

Mexican dictator and military general Antonio López de Santa Anna followed up a spectacular victory with a string of epic failures in 1836. He was fighting in Texas, which was then part of Mexico. He had captured the Alamo on March 6. At that famous fort, every Texan rebel fighting for independence from Mexico died. In the weeks that followed, Santa Anna played cat and mouse with the main Texan army, led by Commander Sam Houston. On April 19, Santa Anna camped his army beside the San Jacinto River. He then made some surprisingly stupid mistakes. He posted no sentries. And he told his soldiers to go ahead and take their usual afternoon naps. On April 21, Houston took advantage of these silly slipups. At 3:30 that afternoon, while the Mexicans napped, he attacked. In a mere 18 minutes, the Texans won a stunning victory. That very bad day for Santa Anna allowed Texas to gain its independence from Mexico.

FAKING OUT THE ENEMY

HANNIBAL— TRICKSTER GENERAL

Unfortunately for Hannibal, most of his elephants died in the cold.

Hannibal was a brilliant military general for Carthage. That city and empire thrived in North Africa in the 200s BC. Hannibal hated the Romans with a passion. So in 218 BC he invaded Roman-controlled Italy. The Romans expected him to land his 30,000 troops on Italy's coast. Taking the land route across the towering, snow-capped Alps was seen as too dangerous. But sure enough, Hannibal crossed the Alps, taking the Romans by surprise. His most daring move? Bringing along his troop of elephants!

Some accounts tell of a near-fatal blunder Hannibal made while crossing the Alps. Frustrated by a slippery path, he reportedly banged his cane on the snow. Bad move! The banging caused an avalanche, burying part of his army.

OOPS!

THE TRAP SHUTS TIGHT

Hannibal then defeated the Romans in battle after battle. His greatest victory came in 216 BC at Cannae, in eastern Italy. The Romans had an enormous army of about 86,000 fighters. They were used to moving straight at an enemy army and capturing its center. The trickster Hannibal turned that rule on its head. He put his best troops in the wings, or sides. As he expected, the Romans charged at his center. At the right moment, Hannibal cleverly ordered his best troops in the wings to attack the center. The trap shut tight on the Romans. Hannibal once again faked the Romans into having a very bad day!

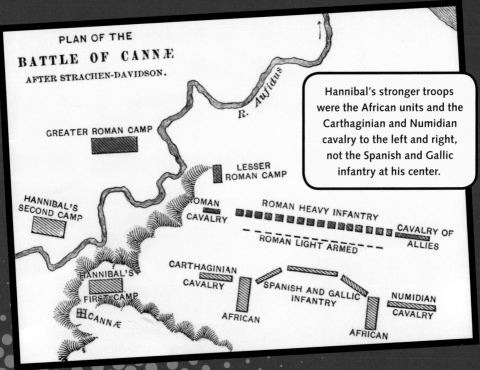

PLAN OF THE

BATTLE OF CANNÆ

AFTER STRACHEN-DAVIDSON.

R. Aufidus

GREATER ROMAN CAMP

LESSER ROMAN CAMP

HANNIBAL'S SECOND CAMP

ROMAN CAVALRY

ROMAN HEAVY INFANTRY

ROMAN LIGHT ARMED

CAVALRY OF ALLIES

HANNIBAL'S FIRST CAMP

CANNÆ

CARTHAGINIAN CAVALRY

SPANISH AND GALLIC INFANTRY

NUMIDIAN CAVALRY

AFRICAN

AFRICAN

Hannibal's stronger troops were the African units and the Carthaginian and Numidian cavalry to the left and right, not the Spanish and Gallic infantry at his center.

FAST FACT

A group of Gauls tried to sneak over Rome's walls in 390 BC. It was nighttime and the Romans were sleeping. But some geese heard the intruders and honked loudly. The Roman guards woke up and fought off the attackers. Foiled by a flock of birds!

FOOLING HITLER

One of the best-known wartime deceptions happened in 1944. It was the height of World War II (1939–1945). That conflict pitted the Allies, including the United States and the United Kingdom, against Germany. The Germans then held most of Europe. The Allies prepared to launch a major invasion from the British Isles. Their real target was Normandy, in northwestern France. Allied commanders wanted to throw the Germans off guard. So they hatched a secret plan to make it look as if the invasion was somewhere else. The Allies created an entire phantom army, the First U.S. Army Group, or FUSAG. To make the con seem real, they chose a famous figure to lead it: U.S. general George S. Patton.

Patton made it look like 1 million soldiers were massing to strike Pas de Calais in northern France instead. Enormous military camps with thousands of tents sprang up like mushrooms across eastern England. What the German spies did not realize was that they were all empty! There were also thousands of jeeps, trucks, and tanks. Most of these were bogus—wooden models or even inflatable rubber fakes! The elaborate trick worked, and German forces were largely fooled. The distraction helped make the Allied invasion of Normandy in June 1944 successful, helping them win the war.

General Patton

One morning in 1944 an English farmer became alarmed. He saw several American tanks parked on his field. Suddenly, one of his bulls charged at one. To the farmer's relief, the animal was unhurt. Its horns penetrated the tank, which made a hissing sound and collapsed. It was only a balloon shaped like a tank!

OOPS!

The tank balloons were so lightweight they could be lifted by just a few soldiers.

DID YOU KNOW?

General Patton believed in reincarnation. He told people he served in a Roman legion and fought for French emperor Napoléon Bonaparte (1769–1821). He also thought he would lead armies again in future lives!

A FAKE FORT

The United Kingdom made inroads into South Africa in the 1800s. The white South African farmers known as Boers saw the British as intruders. They fought several conflicts—the so-called Boer Wars. The Boers heard in 1899 that a British force had taken over the South African town of Mafeking. Eight thousand Boers arrived to take on the enemy and saw that a small fort had been built outside the town. They fired huge numbers of bullets at the fort. Then they captured it. But when they entered the structure, no one was there. It was not even a real fort! Someone had built an empty wooden shell to fool them into wasting bullets.

The Boer forces' large guns were not enough to take the town.

PLAYING THROUGH THE SIEGE

The Boers soon learned who that someone was—Robert Baden-Powell. Britain had sent him to keep the Boers busy for a few months, giving the British a chance to send a bigger army. In the meantime, however, Baden-Powell, his small force, and the people of the town were trapped by the much larger Boer army. The siege lasted seven months as supplies ran out. Baden-Powell organized polo and cricket games to keep up morale. The people trapped in Mafeking kept a stiff upper lip throughout. When the British Army finally arrived, a passerby greeted them with apparent unconcern: "Oh, yes, I heard you were knocking about!"

Robert Baden-Powell went on to found the Boy Scouts in 1907.

DID YOU KNOW?

In the past, women were not allowed to join the army. Some got around this by dressing as men. One of the most famous was Christian Davies, also called Mother Ross. In the 1600s she joined the British Army to search for her husband, who'd been forced to enlist. She swore and swaggered and looted and plundered her way across Europe. When she finally found her husband many years later, she liked army life so much she didn't want to quit!

HOW EMBARRASSING!

WELCOME TO GUAM!

During World War II, the United States fought Japan. The two nations grappled for supremacy in the Pacific Ocean. One by one, American forces took back islands Japan had captured. The U.S. Marines proudly said that they led each attack. But in reality, the Marines were not first, just the first to move in with guns blazing. Before that, underwater demolition teams (UDT) from the U.S. Navy crept onto the beaches. Their mission was to prepare the way for the Marines and other fighters. This extremely dangerous job included mapping out safe routes and clearing away explosive mines.

A UDT instructor leaves the water after training exercises in the U.S. Virgin Islands in 1954.

In July 1944, UDT cleared the target beaches of Guam. When the Marines hit that island's first beach a day later, they found an unexpected gift. It was a homemade sign the UDT had left for them. It read: "Marines, welcome to Guam Beach, open courtesy of UDT!" They were not the first on the scene after all!

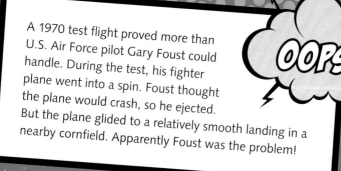

A 1970 test flight proved more than U.S. Air Force pilot Gary Foust could handle. During the test, his fighter plane went into a spin. Foust thought the plane would crash, so he ejected. But the plane glided to a relatively smooth landing in a nearby cornfield. Apparently Foust was the problem!

OOPS!

Enemy general or harmless two-wheeled vehicle?

DID YOU KNOW?

In the 1960s and 1970s, the United States went to war. It fought the southern Asian nation of North Vietnam. At one point, a group of U.S. fighters searched for an enemy supply base. Oddly, they found a shiny red bicycle. The team leader radioed his base and jokingly mentioned capturing a new bike. Not long afterward, several heavily armed U.S. helicopters arrived. It turned out that the base radio operator was using an old codebook. In it, "new bicycle" meant "enemy general!"

THE WAR WON BY BIRDS!

Western Australia witnessed one of the strangest, silliest wars in history in 1932. The locals now call it the Great Emu War. Emus are giant flightless birds that stand taller than a human. They also eat large amounts of plants, including farmers' crops. In fact, it was potential crop losses that triggered the so-called war. That year an estimated 20,000 emus went on an eating rampage. They threatened to destroy hundreds of farmers' fields. Not only would those farmers go out of business, but the local economy would be ruined.

GUNS VERSUS BIRDS

To stop this disaster, the Australian government sent in soldiers armed with machine guns. The first battle involved only about 40 emus. As they approached a farm, the soldiers opened fire. But only a few of the birds fell. The rest sprinted away at amazing speeds and disappeared into a forest! In the next battle, the soldiers ambushed about 100 emus. Almost all of the birds scattered and ran away. In the third encounter, more than 1,000 emus managed to escape the soldiers' guns. People across Australia started joking that the emus were winning the war. So the government called off the army. Big birds for the win!

The emu is the second-largest bird alive. It can top 5 feet (1.5 meters) and 100 pounds (45 kilograms).

The emu and the kangaroo are both shown on the Coat of Arms of Australia. They were chosen because they are the only Australian animals that can't move backward!

JEFFERSON F.

JEFFERSON C.

OOPS!

During the American Civil War (1861–1865), 11 southern states seceded from the United States to form the Confederacy. The president of the Confederacy was Jefferson F. Davis. But there was a Union general named Jefferson C. Davis too. During one battle, some Confederate soldiers approached a group of Union troops saying they were "Jeff Davis' men." The Union soldiers assumed they meant their general and let them pass. The Confederate troops quickly surrounded and captured them!

GOING THE WRONG WAY

GOOGLE'S GOOF

With modern maps and satellites, modern armies ought to know where they are. But countries invade each other by accident more often than you'd think. One "invasion" took place in November 2010. Soldiers from the Central American nation of Nicaragua crossed the border into Costa Rica. On tiny Calero Island they planted the Nicaraguan flag. That small river island has belonged to Costa Rica for more than a century. The soldiers were misled, however, by a simple error. They referred to Google Maps rather than official charts. The newest Google map goofed by placing Calero Island in Nicaraguan territory. So the soldiers thought they were justified in occupying the island. Google soon admitted its error. The soldiers went home, ending the miniature invasion.

The famous Rock of Gibraltar lies in British territory.

FAST FACT

Another military border breach took place in 2002. Twenty British marines guided their landing craft onto a Spanish beach. They thought they were in Gibraltar, a British territory that shares a border with Spain. They realized their error fairly quickly. But the press got wind of it and splashed it across headlines around the world. With a smile, many reporters called it a mini-invasion!

NOT SO NEUTRAL?

Another accidental border violation happened in 2007. Switzerland is famously known for staying neutral in international conflicts. It was surprising, therefore, when 170 Swiss soldiers marched into Liechtenstein, Switzerland's tiny neighbor. Some of the local citizens may have wondered if it was an invasion. But it was just a silly slipup. While on a training mission, the soldiers got lost in the rain and ambled over the border by accident!

WHERE DID THEY GO?

It is hard to fight the enemy if you cannot find them. One of the best-known cases of losing the other army happened in the American Civil War. The battle of Shiloh was fought in Tennessee in April 1862. The first day of fighting went badly for the Union. The Confederates drove General Ulysses S. Grant's soldiers nearly into the Tennessee River. Grant needed reinforcements. So he sent word to General Lew Wallace. Wallace and his 6,500 troops were located 5 miles (8 kilometers) upstream of the main battle. They immediately gathered their weapons and set out, hoping to save the day.

But when they arrived, they found only a vacant field. It was strewn with bodies. Clearly the main fighting had moved somewhere else. Wallace did his best to find the location of the ongoing battle. He led his men on at least two more forced marches. By the time he found Grant, however, the battle was over for the day. Grant blamed Wallace for the Union's losses and nearly ruined Wallace's military reputation.

General Grant, on horseback, tries to hold the Union line at the battle of Shiloh.

Fortunately for Wallace, the failed general later gained a major reputation as an author. His 1880 book, *Ben-Hur*, was a worldwide bestseller. It also became the basis for several Hollywood movies.

Pancho Villa fought against Mexican dictators Porfirio Díaz and Victoriano Huerta.

DID YOU KNOW?

Mexican political figure Pancho Villa became front-page news in March 1916. His followers crossed the U.S. border and killed 17 Americans in a raid on a New Mexico town. U.S. Army general John J. Pershing headed an expedition to bring Villa to justice. Ten thousand people backed Pershing in an 11-month chase. They even took a newfangled invention, the airplane. But all the force of the U.S. Army couldn't find the clever former bandit.

THAT SINKING FEELING

THE TIPPING SHIP

Sweden built the *Vasa* in the 1620s. It was supposed to be one of Europe's strongest warships. A huge crowd gathered in Sweden's capital, Stockholm, in August 1628. All eyes were on the harbor. There, the mighty *Vasa* was set to make its maiden voyage. Large amounts of time and money had gone into its construction. But the ship was in trouble. The king of Sweden had kept changing the orders for the ship as it was built, making it longer and adding guns. It even failed a stability test—but no one knew how to fix it. The navy went ahead with the launch anyway. As the vessel sailed proudly into the open harbor, a strong gust of wind blew in. The ship tipped right over! It sank in only a few minutes.

The salvaged *Vasa* is kept in a Swedish museum dedicated to the ship.

The docks at Nagasaki could handle most immense ships.

MAKING WAVES

Another unexpected run-in with harbor water happened in Nagasaki, Japan. The Japanese readied the *Musashi* for launch in November 1940. It was one of the two largest battleships ever built. But no one foresaw what its enormous bulk would do to the harbor. When the ship entered the water, it set off a small but scary tsunami. That fast-moving wave flooded much of the city!

FAST FACT

Matthew Little was an American sailor. During World War I (1914–1918) and World War II, he served on four different ships. All of them sank, but he managed to survive each time!

THE BIG GOOF

U.S. warship *William D. Porter*, the *Willy D* for short, gained a reputation for being trigger-happy during World War II. This was because of an incredible incident later called the Big Goof. U.S. president Franklin Roosevelt needed to get to Egypt in 1943 for a secret wartime conference. Roosevelt traveled aboard a huge battleship, the USS *Iowa*. The ill-fated *Willy D* was one of the ships that guarded the *Iowa* on its voyage. Everything seemed fine at first. But then the *Willy D*'s captain ordered his crew to stage a training exercise. Something went wrong. The *Willy D* accidentally launched a live torpedo, headed right for the *Iowa*! Fortunately, the *Iowa*'s crew was extremely well trained. They managed to evade the lethal torpedo. The torpedo exploded harmlessly in the water a few minutes later. Thereafter, people in and out of the navy constantly teased the *Willy D*'s crewmen. They were never able to escape being part of the Big Goof, in which they almost assassinated the U.S. president!

The captain and entire crew of the *Willy D* (foreground) were arrested and held in Bermuda until the navy figured out what happened.

Submarine toilets are complicated. During World War II, a German U-boat captain didn't follow the procedure and flushed the toilet wrong. A specialist came to repair the toilet but opened the wrong pipe valve, flooding the vessel. The captain was forced to surface, where the Allies promptly captured him and his men.

Cao Cao is a classic villain in Chinese literature, but historians see him as a talented general and politician.

One of history's biggest bullies was Chinese general Cao Cao of the kingdom of Wei. In the year AD 208 he attacked several neighboring kingdoms. As told in a classic Chinese novel, a spy tricked Cao Cao. He told the general he could cure the sailors' seasickness by chaining his ships together. With the ships unable to maneuver, the defenders easily set them all on fire. The power-hungry but gullible Cao Cao was defeated.

OOPS!

ODD DAYS IN WAR

DON'T TOUCH THAT MONUMENT!

The people of Greece were fighting for their independence in the 1830s. The Turks had controlled Greece for several centuries. Toward the conflict's end, a group of Turkish fighters occupied the Acropolis. This rocky hill in central Athens was already world famous. There, the ancient Athenians had erected several temples, including the renowned Parthenon.

The Greek fighters tried to drive the Turks out of that temple's majestic ruins. But the Turks hung on. Eventually, the Turks ran out of bullets. They became desperate for metal to make new ones. So they attacked the temple's columns. The Turks started digging out the metal clamps that held the columns' stone blocks together. Horrified, the Greeks resorted to their own desperate move. They sent thousands of bullets to the Turks inside the temple. The Greeks attached a note. It read: "Here are bullets. Don't touch the columns!"

The Parthenon towers over the city of Athens on a high hill.

THE PLANE THAT FLEW ITSELF

Another strange military happening occurred in 1989. The Russian air force was conducting training flights in Poland. Suddenly one plane suffered equipment failure. Thinking it would crash, the pilot ejected. He parachuted safely to the ground. But instead of crashing, his plane kept on going! Automated controls kept it flying on and on. The pilotless aircraft traveled all the way across Europe. Finally it crashed in Belgium. Talk about flying on autopilot!

The plane that crashed, a Soviet MiG 23, is also known as a Flogger.

FAST FACT

One of history's oddest battles happened in Egypt in 525 BC. As funny as it sounds, the Egyptians were defeated by pets. The invaders from Persia knew the Egyptians held cats and dogs sacred. So the Persians placed hundreds of those creatures in their front line. Sure enough, the Egyptians were reluctant to fight and lost the battle.

THE BEAR THAT HELPED WIN WORLD WAR II

Certainly one of the weirdest and most amusing stories from modern warfare is that of a member of the Polish army. His name was Wojtek (pronounced VOY-tek), but he was no ordinary soldier. He was a brown bear! This fantastic tale began with a group of Polish fighters in 1942. The Germans had recently overrun their country. So the Poles decided to fight for the British and Americans. While marching through Syria to join the British, the Poles found a cute bear cub. They named it Wojtek, meaning "smiling warrior." The cuddly creature became their mascot. But Wojtek proved to be more than just a furry sidekick. His Polish friends gave him an official soldier's serial number and rank. He even did some soldiers' jobs! During a battle in 1944, he carried heavy mortar shells from the supply trucks to his military buddies in the front lines. Following the war, the story of the noble animal's exploits spread far and wide. Many people thought it humorous that Germany was defeated partly by the efforts of a Polish bear!

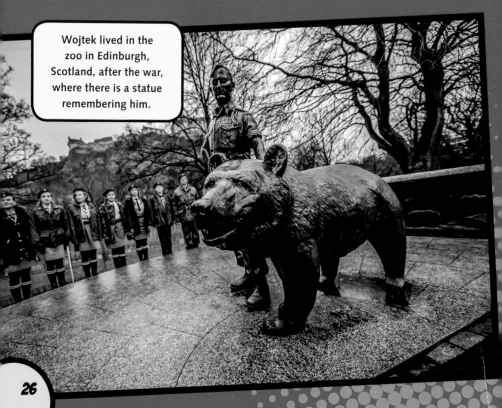

Wojtek lived in the zoo in Edinburgh, Scotland, after the war, where there is a statue remembering him.

DID YOU KNOW?

"Mad Jack" was a British soldier who fought in World War II. His real name was John Churchill. He became known for his odd choice of weapons. He knew how to fire a rifle. But like the warriors of olden times, he preferred his trusty longbow and claymore sword. During the 1940 battle of Dunkirk, Mad Jack actually slew a German soldier with an arrow!

Brač, Yugoslavia: the last man standing after an assault, plays the bagpipes until he's captured (he soon escapes)

Dunkirk, France: leads an attack with a longbow and shoots a German sergeant

1940 1941 1943 1944

Italy: with one other soldier, launches sneak attacks on German posts using his claymore and captures more than 40 enemy fighters

Vågsøy Island, Norway: plays the bagpipes, throws a grenade, then charges the enemy with a claymore sword

FAST FACT

The soldiers of Wojtek the Bear's unit wanted to honor him for his service. They created a new official badge for their unit. It showed an image of the bear holding an artillery shell.

AND HE SURVIVED!

DON'T LEAVE ME HANGING!

Sometimes death seems certain in wartime. But the history of war is filled with amazing and unexpected tales of survival. One of those remarkable people was Gerard of Avesnes. Gerard was a follower of the French lord Godfrey of Bouillon. He fought in Palestine during the First Crusade (1095–1099). The Crusaders were European Christians who saw Palestine as the Holy Land. Muslims had captured Palestine, and the Crusaders wanted to win it back.

Godfrey and his troops besieged the town of Arsuf in 1099. During the fighting, Gerard was captured. The Muslim defenders hung him on a tall wooden mast on the city's front wall. Gerard feared for his life. He called out to Godfrey to halt the siege. But Godfrey refused. When the main assault took place, 12 stray arrows pierced poor Gerard's body. Everyone assumed he was dead. But they were wrong. The human pin cushion survived!

Artist Gustave Doré imagined Gerard's time on the post in an 1877 engraving.

During the Vietnam War, U.S. soldier Billy Campbell took a gunshot to his chest. He should have been a goner. But he was unhurt. The bullet bounced off a spoon he was carrying in his breast pocket.

DO THE WAVE

Robert Goehring served aboard the Coast Guard cutter USS *Duane* during World War II. During a storm at sea, a huge wave swept him off the boat. His shipmates figured he was gone for good. But with some quick thinking, they maneuvered the boat closer and waited. The next wave heaved him up alongside the ship, where the other sailors grabbed him. Talk about catching a wave!

The USS *Duane* navigated heavy seas in the North Atlantic Ocean during World War II.

BAD ORDERS

FROM LEADER TO LAUGHINGSTOCK

Sometimes the biggest military mistakes involve bad orders. Typically they come from inept or cowardly commanders. A perfect example was the spineless bungler Gideon Pillow. Pillow first showed his bad judgment during the Mexican-American War (1846–1848). President James K. Polk was an old friend. During the war he made Pillow a military general. The Americans won several major battles over the Mexicans. Pillow had nothing to do with these victories. Yet he bragged they were his doing! That made him very unpopular in army circles.

This cartoon makes fun of General Pillow for puffing up his military record. He is kneeling and blowing up a pillow filled with air as another general punctures it with a sword labeled "truth."

POLK'S PATENT Self-Inflating PILLOW.

Heavens what a smell!

Major Bur
U.S.A.

NOWHERE TO HIDE

General Pillow's most famous blunder occurred in 1863, at the height of the American Civil War. Pillow was an officer for the Confederacy. In the battle of Stones River, he was ordered to lead his men against the Union force. But he was nowhere to be seen. One of his superior officers, Major General John C. Breckenridge, set out to find him. Breckenridge soon discovered Pillow hiding behind a tree. When word got out, the southerners were terribly embarrassed. But northerners thought it was hilarious.

NOT MUSIC FANS

Britain's Charles MacCarthy issued orders that were even more inept. He was governor of a British colony in Africa in 1824. The Ashanti, a local tribe, opposed the British. So MacCarthy led his army against them. Because the Ashanti were black, in his racist worldview, he reasoned they must be backward and cowardly. "Civilized" music would therefore scare them away. He ordered his band to play "God Save the King." This move naturally failed. The 10,000 Ashanti warriors proceeded to kill most of the 600 British, including MacCarthy.

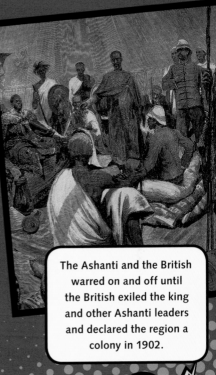

The Ashanti and the British warred on and off until the British exiled the king and other Ashanti leaders and declared the region a colony in 1902.

General Pillow is known for yet another blunder. During the Mexican-American War, he built a fort at the village of Camargo. Typically an army will dig a ditch outside the wall of a fort. This makes the wall harder for the enemy to climb. But Pillow had the brilliant idea to dig the ditch on the inside—where anyone who made it to the top of the wall could easily jump over it!

OOPS!

SELF-PROMOTION

Some people should never have been trusted to lead troops. James Wilkinson was one of them. His career began during the U.S. Revolutionary War (1775–1783) as a captain in the Continental Army. He puffed up his role in the battle of Saratoga in the official report. He was sent to deliver the report to the Continental Congress. He, along with his girlfriend, took his time on the way, angering Congress. Yet he got himself promoted over more qualified officers.

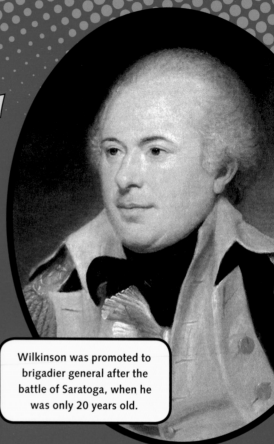

Wilkinson was promoted to brigadier general after the battle of Saratoga, when he was only 20 years old.

DID YOU KNOW?

Every president from George Washington to James Madison suspected that Wilkinson was a spy. They thought he was passing secrets to the Spanish, but no one could pin him down. He even weathered several trials and was found not guilty each time. But two centuries after his death, historians uncovered documents proving he did it.

TOTAL INCOMPETENCE

Between wars, in 1809, Wilkinson was in charge of approximately 2,000 troops stationed near New Orleans, Louisiana. He set up camp in a swamp to be near the city and its entertainments. But he lost half his army to disease and desertion. This was the largest peacetime loss of men in the U.S. Army of that era. During the next war, the War of 1812, his continuing incompetence caused the death of many men under him. He also failed to defeat a British force half the size of his.

Scotland's Lord Robert Maxwell made a mess of things in 1542. That year a force of close to 18,000 Scottish soldiers gathered to attack northern England. Initially, Maxwell was in charge. The Scots faced a mere 3,000 English troops. But in the battle of Solway Moss, Maxwell failed to take charge. His men received no orders, fell into chaos, and the English won!

OOPS!

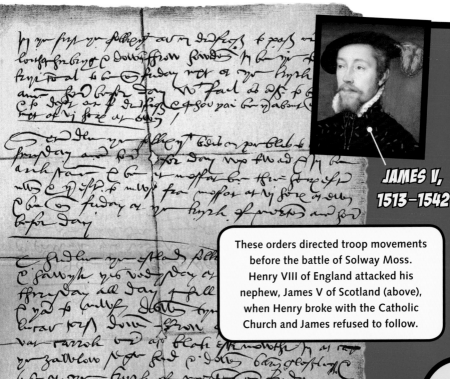

JAMES V, 1513–1542

These orders directed troop movements before the battle of Solway Moss. Henry VIII of England attacked his nephew, James V of Scotland (above), when Henry broke with the Catholic Church and James refused to follow.

HORSE VERSUS TANK

It might be hard to imagine a major modern nation having completely unskilled and unqualified military generals. Yet this was the case in the Soviet Union in the late 1930s. At the outbreak of World War II in 1939, the Soviet army had several very bad generals. But two stand out for their refusal to accept the idea of progress. Semyon Budyonny had been a cavalry commander in World War I. Charging the enemy on horseback would never be surpassed, he said. Even in the 1930s he condemned the use of tanks, missiles, and warplanes. Budyonny's blindness to progress led to big-time disaster. He led a huge Soviet army against invading German forces in 1941. Suddenly he faced thousands of the tanks and planes he had dismissed. These quickly overwhelmed him. The Germans were easily able to surround his army, which suffered huge losses.

Budyonny left the military and became a horse breeder after the war.

NO NEW GUNS!

As military nitwits go, Budyonny's comrade, General Grigory Kulik, was not far behind. Kulik was another throwback to old-time warfare. He, too, thought cavalry charges were more effective than tanks. Yet somehow in 1935 he was put in charge of developing artillery! It was at least partly his fault that the Soviets had older tanks and guns when they joined World War II a few years later.

DID YOU KNOW?

Sometimes even talented military leaders fail. The ancient Greek king Pyrrhus was an example. He repeatedly defeated the Romans in the 280s BC. But he lost many soldiers in the process. Embarrassed, he made an ironic statement that is now famous: "One more victory like that over the Romans will destroy us completely!" Since then, winning a battle at high cost has been called a Pyrrhic victory.

Pyrrhus died in a skirmish in 272 BC.

MISTAKEN IDENTITY

GIVE PEACE A CHANCE

The Cold War of the mid-20th century pitted the democratic West against the communist Soviet powers after World War II ended. Russia was still the Soviet Union and Germany was divided into East and West. During this tense time, an everyday citizen of West Germany, Mathias Rust, outwitted a major nation's entire military. The feat happened in May 1987. Rust wanted to see the whole world at peace. So he composed an essay urging Soviet leader Mikhail Gorbachev to always choose peace over war.

Mathias Rust lands in Red Square in Moscow.

U.S. planes were crossing the Mediterranean Sea en route to Libya on a bombing mission in 1986. Seeing steam rising from the ocean, the pilots assumed they had discovered a Libyan submarine and dropped bombs. But the steam was coming from an underwater volcano. They had actually bombed an underwater island claimed by Italy!

OOPS!

WHO'S FLYING THAT PLANE?

Rust worried that if he simply mailed the essay, it might not get through. So he took off in a small airplane and flew it straight to Moscow, the Soviet capital. The defense units guarding the Soviet border saw his plane. But they thought it was a Russian plane. So they let him through. After that, one by one Rust approached the other Soviet layers of defense. They either assumed he was a local or too small to be a threat. Incredibly he made it through all of them! He finally landed his plane right in Red Square, in Moscow's heart. Soviet authorities were naturally embarrassed. Rust made them a laughingstock around the globe. They arrested him. But people everywhere saw him as a hero.

An American soldier stands guard at a remote Alaskan outpost during World War II.

DID YOU KNOW?

During World War II, the Japanese occupied a small U.S. island. Called Kiska, it is part of Alaska. The Americans bombed the island in 1943. Then more than 30,000 U.S. and Canadian troops assaulted it. After many hours of firing at buildings, they discovered something upsetting. The island was empty. The Japanese had all left three weeks before!

WHAT A WAY TO START A WAR!

San Juan Island is one of several islands in the San Juan archipelago.

WHOSE ISLAND IS IT ANYWAY?

Sometimes opposing nations allow their emotions to get the best of them. Something ridiculous then sends them to the brink of war. The Pig War is a perfect example. The United States and the United Kingdom signed a treaty in 1846. It divided up the lands west of the Rocky Mountains. But both parties claimed tiny San Juan Island. It is located near much larger Vancouver Island, now in southwestern Canada.

DID YOU KNOW?

Another silly dispute between the United States and the United Kingdom began in 1838. It came to be called the Aroostook War. Some Americans in Maine cut firewood in an area claimed by both nations. Soldiers from the two countries arrived and faced off. Fortunately, emotions calmed. The two parties settled the dispute, avoiding a bloody war over firewood!

The border between Greece and Bulgaria in 1925 was a hot spot for tempers on both sides. A Greek soldier chased a stray dog across the border. Next a Bulgarian shot the Greek soldier. That ignited a brief, small, but totally needless conflict. It went down in history as the War of the Stray Dog!

GOING THE WHOLE HOG

Some Americans started settling and farming on the island. The British considered this illegal. Tempers on both sides rose. Then, in June 1859, American settler Lyman Cutlar shot and killed a pig that belonged to a British trading company. Cutlar refused to pay for the creature. U.S. troops landed on the island to back him up. Soon after, British warships arrived as well. It appeared that two great nations were about to go to war over a pig! For 12 years the opposing soldiers eyed each other warily. Finally, in 1871, the two countries settled the matter peacefully. San Juan Island became part of the United States. It turned out that the only casualty of the "almost" war over a pig was the unfortunate pig itself!

The pig in question was a champion Berkshire, a valuable animal.

ONE EXPENSIVE BUCKET

War broke out for a foolish reason in 1325. The two nations involved were the northern Italian states of Modena and Bologna. One day some Modenese soldiers walked into Bologna and stole a few valuable items. They carried them away in an oak pail. The Bolognese were outraged. They gathered their army and marched on Modena. The goal was to win back the bucket. To them, it stood for the insult they felt they had endured. The Bolognese army numbered some 32,000 fighters. In contrast, the Modenese had only 7,000 soldiers. The two armies clashed in November 1325. Incredibly, the hugely outnumbered Modenese won the day! The humiliated Bolognese scurried away. The bucket is still on display in Modena today.

The 1325 war was part of a centuries-long conflict between two Italian families, the Ghibellines and the Guelfs, from the 12th through 14th centuries.

Sea birds such as gannets nest closely together on small sea islands, concentrating their guano.

FAST FACT

Chile, Bolivia, and Peru once went to war over bird droppings! Sounds funny, but it actually made sense. When the war started in 1879, guano—accumulated droppings found where birds or bats nest—was an expensive and sought-after fertilizer.

OUCH, MY EAR!

Still another downright stupid reason for a war involved a person's ear. Its owner, Robert Jenkins, was an English sea captain. When he was at sea, some Spanish sailors boarded his ship. They sliced off one of his ears. Unbelievably, he pickled the ear and kept it in a bottle! The British people were outraged over Jenkins' loss. They demanded the Spanish be taught a lesson. This provoked the so-called War of Jenkins' Ear, which erupted in 1739. It resulted in a British fleet capturing a Spanish harbor in the Americas.

FUN FACTS

Mexico's military general Santa Anna lost a leg in a fight against the French in 1838. One of the wooden legs Santa Anna wore after that is presently on display in Illinois's State Military Museum.

Confederate general Nathan Bedford Forrest was born on Friday the Thirteenth in July 1821. During the American Civil War, he had 29 horses shot out from under him, but he lived. Does this make him lucky or unlucky?

Mud has been bogging down armies since the beginning of war. Cavalry charges, tanks and trucks, or simply marching soldiers quickly turn solid soil into mud. Soldiers lose their boots and have to continue in socks. In the Vietnam War, tanks got so stuck that their operators used explosives to free them.

The fake tanks of Wold War II's Operation Fortitude were not heavy enough to leave tracks. There was a chance that German pilots might notice the absence of such tracks. So at night Allied soldiers used special tools to make fake tread marks, a trick that worked!

*I*taly's Ubaldo Soddu would have had a reputation as a great general if World War II had not broken out. He enjoyed the finer things in life—music and pasta—a little too much. He spent his time composing movie sound tracks while the opposing army demolished his troops.

*H*annibal scared the Romans so much that for generations they'd say "Hannibal is at the gates!" whenever something bad happened. Roman parents even used the phrase to frighten children into behaving.

*T*he battle for the Acropolis in the 1830s was not the first time the Turks caused damage to the Parthenon. In 1687, the Turks occupied Athens during a war with the Italian city of Venice. Turkish commanders stored their gunpowder inside the Parthenon, so the Venetians fired their cannons on the structure. It violently exploded, instantly becoming a ruin.

*T*he ancient Egyptians held many animals in high esteem, but none more than cats. These creatures were closely connected to several gods and goddesses, including Bast, seen to have the power of a lioness. In Egyptian eyes, killing a cat was a terrible crime. A Greek author from the first century BC reports that when a Roman visiting Egypt accidentally killed one, a gang of ordinary locals tore him to shreds.

GLOSSARY

Allies (AL-eyez)—alliance of nations that fought Germany and Japan in World War II, including the United States, Britain, and France

artillery (ahr-TIL-ur-ee)—large guns that shoot long distances, or the part of the army that uses such guns

assassinate (uh-SAS-uh-nate)—to kill for political reasons

Boer (BOR)—white South African farmer; Boers fought the British in the 1800s

breach (BREECH)—to violate; or a violation

cavalry (KAV-uhl-ree)—military unit based on horses

codebook (KODE-buk)—in wartime, a list of secret codes used to keep the enemy from understanding one's messages

Confederate (kuhn-FED-ur-it)—in the American Civil War, the states that seceded to form the Confederate States of America, or the South

desertion (di-ZUR-shuhn)— abandoning military service

eject (i-JEKT)—in the case of a pilot, to leave his plane and parachute to the ground

gullible (GUHL-uh-buhl)—easy to fool

incompetence (in-KAHM-pi-tuhnts)—uselessness, stupidity, or lack of skill

mascot (MAS-kaht)—an animal or something else that a group chooses as their official sign

medieval (mee-DEE-vuhl)—pertaining to the Middle Ages, the roughly thousand-year-long period that occurred after ancient times and before modern times

mine (MINE)—in wartime, a bomb planted in the ground or water

phantom (FAN-tuhm)—a ghost or unreal person

tsunami (tsu-NAH-mee)—a large, powerful, and potentially destructive sea wave

Union (YOON-yuhn)—in the American Civil War, the United States of America, or the North

FIND OUT MORE

BOOKS

Lucas, Bill. *History's Greatest Military Mistakes Close-up*. New York: Rosen, 2015.

Nicholson, Dorinda. *Remembering World War II: Kids Who Survived Tell Their Stories*. Washington, D.C.: National Geographic, 2015.

Perritano, John, and James Spears. *National Geographic Kids Everything Battles: Arm Yourself with Fierce Photos and Fascinating Facts*. Washington, D.C.: National Geographic, 2013.

PLACES TO VISIT

American Civil War Museum
500 Tredegar Street
Richmond, Virginia 23219
https://acwm.org/
The mission of The American Civil War Museum is to explore the American Civil War and its legacies from multiple perspectives: Union and Confederate, enslaved and free African Americans, and soldiers and civilians.

National WWII Museum
945 Magazine Street
New Orleans, Louisiana 70130
http://www.nationalww2museum.org/
The National WWII Museum tells the story of the American experience in the war that forever changed the world, including why it was fought, how it was won, and what it means today.

FURTHER RESEARCH

Battles sometimes have unexpected long-term consequences. In May 1905, for example, during the Russo-Japanese War, the Japanese defeated the Russians in the huge sea battle of Tsushima. Look online under the battle's "aftermath" to see how this victory contributed to the outbreak of World War II more than 30 years later.

The American Civil War introduced so many military innovations that some historians call it the first modern war. For example, three Louisiana residents—James McClintock, Baxter Watson, and Horace L. Hunely—got together to create the first military submarine. Look them up online to find the details.

WEBSITES

FactHound offers a safe, fun way to find Internet sites related to this book. All of the sites on FactHound have been researched by our staff.

Here's all you do:

Visit *www.facthound.com*

Type in this code: 9781410985620

Super-cool stuff!

Check out projects, games and lots more at
www.capstonekids.com

INDEX